First published in 2013

Allen & Unwin
83 Alexander Street
Crows Nest NSW 2065
Australia
Phone: (61 2) 8425 0100
Email: info@allenandunwin.com
Web: www.allenandunwin.com

A Cataloguing-in-Publication entry is available
from the National Library of Australia
www.trove.nla.gov.au

ISBN 978 174175 887 0

Kim Gamble used watercolour for the artwork in this book.

Cover design by Sandra Nobes
Set in Old Claude by Tou-Can Design
Colour reproduction by Splitting Image, Clayton, Victoria.
This book was printed in July 2013 at Everbest Printing Co Ltd
in 334 Huanshi Road South, Nansha, Guangdong, China

10 9 8 7 6 5 4 3 2 1

Once Tashi Met a Dragon

ANNA FIENBERG *and*
BARBARA FIENBERG
pictures by KIM GAMBLE

ALLEN & UNWIN
SYDNEY · MELBOURNE · AUCKLAND · LONDON

Ever since he could remember, Tashi had been
told stories about the dragon. Grandmother said the
dragon lived over the mountain and far away.
Second Uncle said the dragon lived in a palace of
gold – he'd seen it once with his telescope, twinkling
like a star. Wise-as-an-Owl said they'd be lucky
if they *never* saw a dragon in their whole lives.

But everyone agreed that it was the dragon
who brought the rains. Once a year,
smoke and thunder came spilling down
the mountain and into the village.

'That'll be the dragon, simmering away like a great pot on the boil,' Grandmother said. 'Don't worry, Tashi, he's cooking up rain – big lashing whooping roaring rains that wash away all the dirt and dullness of the year, and make the air sparkle like a million diamonds. That's what a dragon does for you.'

Until one year, when Tashi had grown up to his father's waist, the rains didn't come. The rice blackened in the fields and the sun's heat lay thick as a blanket over the land.

'Maybe the dragon is dead?' Luk Ahed, the fortune teller, wondered, consulting his charts.

Grandmother didn't think so. 'Dragons live almost forever.'

Wise-as-an-Owl was worried.
'Nobody knows how old our dragon
is. Nobody has ever dared climb
up the mountain to see.'

Just then, a forest of pines exploded
like firecrackers. Smoke rose into
a cloud that floated to the top
of the mountain and stayed there.
'Good,' said Luk Ahed. 'He's awake. Soon the rains will come.'

But the skies stayed blue.
The air crackled, fires flew, and the earth turned to dust.
'Something has to be done,' Tashi said to Lotus Blossom.
'But what?'

The next day, when Tashi and Lotus Blossom were walking
along a dry creek bed, they stopped short. A bedraggled
white tiger was lying under the willow tree.
'Could I trouble you for a sip of water?' the tiger asked politely.
'I haven't had a good drink for days.'

Tashi poured water from his flask into the tiger's mouth. He gulped it down so eagerly that Lotus Blossom added hers. When the tiger had finished, Tashi asked how his tail came to be burnt.

'It got caught in dragon fire,' said the tiger.

'Oh! Have you seen the dragon?' asked Lotus Blossom.

'Why doesn't he bring the rains?'

The tiger shook his head. '*She*. The old dragon is a *she*. And it's not the old dragon who's starting these fires. It's that young one, Tum-tum, her boy. He hasn't yet learnt Flame Management. And he's angry that his mother has fallen asleep and won't wake up.'

Tashi and Lotus Blossom looked at each other.
'Wah!' said Tashi. '*Two* dragons! What else do you
know about them?'

'Well,' said the tiger, 'one thing I know for certain,
there is nothing dragons are afraid of, except demons.'
'*Everyone's* afraid of demons,' shuddered Lotus Blossom.
'Yes,' said the tiger. 'But demons can steal into a dragon's
dream and never leave.'

'Oh!' cried Tashi. 'I met a demon once, but I didn't look into its eyes because you can get trapped in a demon trance forever.' He thought for a moment. 'Dear Tiger, could you possibly show us the way up the mountain to see these dragons?'

The tiger said yes he could, and in return for their kindness, he could take one of them on his back. Tashi looked at Lotus Blossom. 'Oh, that's all right,' said Lotus Blossom quickly. 'You go, Tashi. I'll run back and tell Grandmother what's happened. Good luck!'

So Tashi rode on the tiger's back, over the fields, through the forest, up to the top of the mountain where only dragons live. 'I will leave you here, Tashi,' said the tiger. 'When the young dragon comes back, don't show yourself. Speak to him gently to gain his trust, or he will eat you as soon as look at you.'

Tashi crouched down amongst the bushes and waited.
Under his knees the ground was baking hot. The only sounds
were the breeze in the trees and a rumbling snore. He peeped
through the leaves and blinked at the cave with its golden
palace glowing above, just as Second Uncle had said.

Suddenly, there was the thunder-snap of wings.
A dragon flew down and stopped right outside the cave.

'Mamma, I'm home. Are you awake? Please come
out to play, it's so boring by myself all day!' There was no reply,
only a rumbling snore and the breeze in the trees.

The young dragon sat down *blumf* on the ground.
A tear splashed onto his tummy. He sang softly to himself.

'Here I sit, so sad and lonely, all I can think is…if *only*,
If only I hadn't ate my sister
No one said how much I'd miss her.'

The young dragon sighed and a bush near Tashi burst into flames.

He leapt away and fell right at the dragon's feet.
'Ooah, what are you?' cried the dragon. 'Are you friend or food?
Maybe I should taste you, just to see.'
'No!' Tashi said. 'You've had far too much to eat already.
And if you swallowed me you'd have no one to talk to.
Wouldn't you rather have company?'

'Yes, I would,' said the dragon.
He put his head in his wings and began to rock.
'I feel so desolate, depressed and doomed,
My mother's asleep,
my sister consumed...'

'Would you like to hear a story to take your mind off your
troubles?' asked Tashi. 'I've had many adventures in my time.
Once I was captured by a witch and nearly baked in her oven...'
'Ooh no, too scary!'

'Well, once I was
captured by the river pirate
and nearly became his slave...'

'Ooh no, I don't like pirates –
all those swords and swearing.'

'Well once I was nearly
hypnotized by demons–'
The dragon leapt up
and towered over Tashi.

'*Demons!* Demons are the worst!
They steal our treasure and...and...
Ooh, my mother will be
in a demon sleep forever!'
Tum-tum began to cry
as if he'd never stop.

'Poor you,' said Tashi.
'Tell me, what does your mother do when you hurt yourself?'
'She wraps me up in her wings.'

'What else?' said Tashi.

'She sings me a special song.'

'Well, I think you should sing that right now, and you'll feel better.'

'No!' cried Tum-tum. 'Mother said it's our *secret* song.

It belongs to us only.'

'Your mother didn't know you would be left so lonely,' Tashi said.

'When *I'm* sad, I sing a song my mother taught me.'

The dragon looked at Tashi. He took a deep breath.

'*We are dragons of fire bright,*
Of thunder, rain and deep moonlight.
We're old as the earth when the earth was new
Winging through forests wet with dew.

'*Come now, my child, and sing with me*
Of shiny jewels and the sparkling sea.
We'll breathe our fire, we'll smite our foe
And 'neath our rains, the fields will grow...'

At the last word,
a snore from the darkness grew into a roar
and suddenly the door of the cave was filled with dragon.
Newly woken, fire-breathing, outraged dragon.

'Mummy!'
'Tum-tum!'

The dragons nosed each other and then the old dragon saw Tashi.
'Who is this?' she said fiercely. 'Has he hurt you?'
'No,' said Tum-tum. 'It was Tashi who told me to sing our song,
and that's what woke you up.'

'The demon sleep!' roared the old dragon.
'Our treasure will be gone.' She shook her head, and blinked.
'Never mind, *you* are still here, my love.
And what have you done with your sister?'
'I ate her.'

The old dragon groaned. 'Oh, Tum-tum, you must *think* before
you act, aren't I always telling you? I can see I'm going to have
to teach you Dragon Lore, my dear. Rule number one: never,
ever eat your sister. Rule number two: if you do happen to eat
her, you must stand on your horns, sing our song backwards,
open your mouth wide, and out she will come.'

And that is what the young dragon did.
There was an enormous explosion that
shook the ground beneath their feet,
and out flew a small dragon,
hot and crumpled and cross.

'That's better,' said the old dragon.
'Now I must grant this Tashi person
a dragon wish for his trouble. What will it be?'
Tashi stared at the family of dragons. He shook his head, dazed.
'What we really need is rain. Could you please send the rains?'
'Yes, and show *me* how!' cried Little Sister.
'And me too!' cried Tum-tum.
The old dragon lifted her head,
shooting a single flame into the sky.

She gathered her children around her.
'Listen well now,' she told them. And from her dragon mouth
wisps of dragon words blew into the air and bloomed into black
balloons that burst against the sky. And with the words came the
lashing whooping roaring rains that ran down the mountainside,
filling the creeks and flowing into the river.

'Now I will take you back
to your family,' the old dragon said.
She settled Tashi on her back and they flew over the fields,
across the river and safely back home, where Grandmother
and Lotus Blossom and Wise-as-an-Owl were laughing with joy,
their arms lifted to the sparkling sky.